pitter pattern

Joyce Hesselberth

Greenwillow Books
An Imprint of HarperCollinsPublishers

Pitter, pitter, pat! Pitter, pitter, pat! Pitter, pitter, pat!
Hey, it's a pitter, pitter pattern!

Lu helps her friends
take off their wet things.

Boot, boot, puddle.
Boot, boot, puddle.
Another pattern!

What comes next?

Boot, boot, puddle.

Milk, apple, cracker, cheese.
Milk, apple, cracker, cheese.
Milk, apple, cracker, cheese.

There are patterns everywhere!
How many can you find?

After snack time, Lu says goodbye to her friends.
She'll see them again next Sunday.

Next Sunday?

Hey, the days of the week are a pattern too!

Thursday

Friday

Saturday

And then it starts again.

Monday

Lu has soccer practice after school on Monday.
She and her teammates practice kicking the
ball between the cones.

In, out. In, out. In, out.

Soccer balls are made of black and white shapes that fit together.

These shapes curve around the entire ball.

D E F G A B C D E F G A E

On Tuesday Lu goes to her piano lesson.
Hey, look at the piano keys!
Two black keys, three black keys,
two black keys, three black keys,
all the way up the keyboard.

Tuesday

The notes on the white keys
are a pattern too.
A, B, C, D, E, F, G,
A, B, C, D, E, F, G.

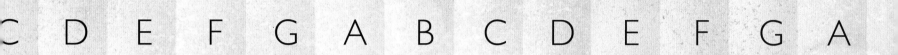

C D E F G A B C D E F G A

Lu claps her hands together
to learn the rhythm of the song.
Ta, ti-ti, ta-ah-ah-ah.
Ta, ti-ti, ta-ah-ah-ah.

Music is full of patterns.

Wednesday

Jump	Hop	Kick	Twirl

Jump	Hop	Kick	Twirl

In dance class, the beat of the drum is a pattern.

Boom, ba-ba, boooom. Boom, ba-ba, boooom.

And the steps in Lu's dance make a pattern.

Jump Hop Kick Twirl

Jump Hop Kick Twirl

What a nice day!
Lu and her dad go for a walk in the park.
Are there patterns here?

And here?

Friday

Lu spends Friday night with her grandma.

They curl up in quilts and read a story.

The patterns in the quilts all have names . . .

evening star,

pinwheels,

attic windows,

and Lu's favorite—**flying geese.**

When the story is over, it's time for bed.

It's hard to fall asleep.
Counting sheep might help.

White sheep, white sheep, black sheep.
White sheep, white sheep, black sheep.

Shzzzz shzzzz shzzzz . . .

The next morning, Lu and her grandma ride the bus to the zoo.

Are
there
patterns
here?

And here?

Lu loves all the animals she saw today.
She can't wait to tell her friends about them, on . . .

Sunday!

Pitter, pitter, pat! Pitter, pitter, pat! Pitter, pitter, pat!

What is a pattern?

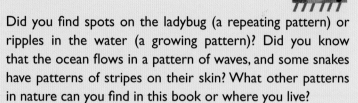

A pattern is a design that's predictable. It's often something that repeats. We use patterns to help predict what comes next and to help us understand how the world works.

Different kinds of patterns

There are many kinds of patterns in the natural world and in the man-made world, too. Here are some of the patterns that Lu discovered during her week:

Repeating patterns

AABAAB

Repeating patterns are always the same. The core of the pattern is the part that repeats. For example, if the pattern is **AABAAB**, then the core is **AAB**.

Growing patterns

1, 2, 3, 4, 5

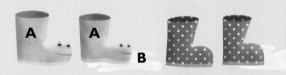

Growing patterns increase or decrease by the same amount each time. You can think about a growing pattern as an addition or subtraction rule. For example, if the pattern is **2, 4, 6** and the rule is that you add 2 each time, what comes next? **2, 4, 6 ... 8**!

Where did Lu find patterns?

In nature

Did you find spots on the ladybug (a repeating pattern) or ripples in the water (a growing pattern)? Did you know that the ocean flows in a pattern of waves, and some snakes have patterns of stripes on their skin? What other patterns in nature can you find in this book or where you live?

In shapes, colors, and pictures

The soccer balls have a pattern of pentagons and hexagons. Grandma's quilts are made of triangles and squares that fit together to repeat the same way each time. What patterns do you see in Lu's house?

In time

The days of the week are a pattern. Lu knows what will happen each day because her schedule is a pattern. Soccer practice is always on Monday, for example. You can also find patterns in hours, months, and years. What is the pattern of your week?

 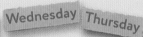

In music and dance

Lu found patterns in the keys of the piano and the rhythms of music. She also danced in a pattern: jump, hop, kick, twirl. Can you invent a dance that is a pattern?

In weather

Does it always rain on Sunday? No, but you can find many patterns in weather. These patterns might be different and they depend on where you live. In Lu's town, there are lots of rainy days in the spring!

To three of my favorite people
who love to play in the rain:
Madison, Emma, and Jacob

Pitter Pattern

Copyright © 2020 by Joyce Hesselberth

All rights reserved. Manufactured in China. For information address HarperCollins Children's Books,
a division of HarperCollins Publishers, 195 Broadway, New York, NY 10007.
www.harpercollinschildrens.com

Watercolors, acrylic paint, gouache, and digital collage were used to create the illustrations. The text type is Gill Sans.

Library of Congress Cataloging-in-Publication Data

Names: Hesselberth, Joyce, author, illustrator. Title: Pitter pattern / Joyce Hesselberth.
Description: First edition. | New York, NY : Greenwillow Books, an imprint of HarperCollinsPublishers, [2020] | Summary: Lu and her
friends spot patterns in their daily activities, including patterns found in music, weather, time, play, shapes, nature, math, and language.
Identifiers: LCCN 2019018974 | ISBN 9780062741233 (hardback)
Subjects: | CYAC: Pattern perception—Fiction.
Classification: LCC PZ7.1.H53 Pi 2020 | DDC [E]—dc23 LC record available at https://lccn.loc.gov/2019018974

19 20 21 22 23 SCP 10 9 8 7 6 5 4 3 2 1
First Edition
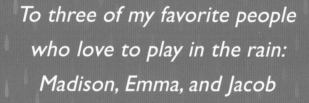
Greenwillow Books